To Kar

UPWARDS

POETRY

by

Piers Rowlandson

for Pier
March 2023

ISBN 9798378299638

Imprint: independently published

Author's note: For obvious reasons it is important to state that all the people and incidents in this book of poetry are imaginary.

Photographs on the front and back covers are by Kim Rowlandson. The others photos are by the author unless otherwise stated.

Dedication
To my children and grandchildren.
Upwards and onwards
my brave explorers.

Brave Explorers

Hey ho and up we go,
my brave explorers.
Don't look down,
and don't look up;
keep your eyes on the prize:
the far mountain top,
if you reach it or if you don't,
only you will know;
like Mallory and Irvine;
only they will ever know
if they reached the top.
For you it's the same,
only you will know,
(and I will know
because I love you).

Bluebell Woods

It is easy to ignore
the humble daisy
when viewing bluebells.

Children
will be making daisy chains
long after the bluebells

have withered away.

The constant daisy,
the fleeting bluebell.
Which one are you?

Cousin/Cousine

At family gatherings,
we kiss.
Right cheek, left cheek,
or,
left and then right?
She goes one way,
I go the other.
Our lips touch and
we rub noses,
like eskimos.

Living next door to Alice.

St Valentine's Eve.
The girl across the avenue,
is in her bedroom.
She has not drawn her curtains.
She's called Alice.
I spit out the pips,
one at a time:
she loves me,
she loves me not.
Damn.
Anyway,
who the fuck is Alice?

Sacha
or
Perfection

She was a perfect animal.
The first thing you noticed were her green eyes.
They had gold flecks that lit up in sunlight.
They flashed when she was angry
and changed to grey when she was sad.
Then there was her scent:
musky, salty like the Mediterranean.
I can't describe it.
It made the hairs on the back of your neck stand up.
It made you want her
but at the same time it made you afraid of her.
It was an evening in June.
I called round to take her to the pub,
the one surrounded by a flowering meadow
on the banks of the Cherwell.
She was painting her toenails green.
She was completely naked
but that did not bother her at all.
She was as comfortable in her skin as a panther.
"Je suis une force qui va!" she once told me.
"Victor Hugo was a man," I said,
"and you are not a man."
She smiled.
"I could be," she said.
"I could be anything."

The Pine Trees

The wind in the pines
recalls the roar of the waves
on a shingle beach.

Brighton Days,
sunbathing by the Angel.
"Pass the suntan cream, Sacha."

Remembering Sacha

The blind is drawn down.
I approach the figure in the bed.
He doesn't move
but seems to sense my approach.
I hear him murmur
"Sacha?"
"No, it's Emma," I tell him.
"It's time for your injection."
"The last one, do you think?" he asks.
I can't answer that:
he is so near the end.
"I thought I heard her," he says.
"There's no-one here by that name," I say.
"No."
There is a long pause before he goes on:
"Do you know the last thing she said to me?"
I shake my head.
I'm not sure he can see me;
there is hardly any light in the room.
He carries on:
"I'm going to make a bid for freedom.
That just about sums it up, don't you think?"
I can see him smiling.
"I do hope I'll see her again," he says.

Reach for the Sky

Photo by John Green, Cowes.

Reach for the sky.
Per ardua ad astra.
The narrow winding road over the Downs,
from the sparkling sea to the dark woods.
It's a long road,
but you'll make it.
You will reach the stars.
"And then?" you'll ask.
But I have nothing more to say.

The Odeon Cinema
Midhurst
1959
(now a supermarket)
is where we saw:
Reach for the Sky,
Battle of the River Plate,
Sink the Bismarck.
Heroic war films,
but the man
who took us small boys
to the cinema
never mentioned
his brother
killed in action,
Sicily,
13th July 1943.

The regret and the sorrow,
the guilt of the survivor,
is expressed in silence.
The put-it-to-the-back-of-your-mind memory,
to be recalled in quiet hours,
while fishing,
while sitting by the river,
while watching the float
on the untroubled waters of a pool,
surrounded by overhanging trees.
Not weeping,

but struggling to bring back
the beloved face,
the ready smile,
the familiar voice.
Fading sepia memories.

The Gate into the Churchyard

It's called a kissing gate,
she remembered.
Leaning over it
she gave
the long gone,
long lost boy
a kiss.
-§-
In the churchyard
she stood before
the plain grey stone.
In loving memory
He led the way
We can only follow
-§-
She stooped
to lay
a bunch
of small blue flowers
among
the weeds
and the long unkempt grass.
My love, my love, she murmured.
Tears trickled down her face.

Apple Blossom Time
A dialogue

Rick: Remember the orchard?

Diana: The apple blossom?

R: But before the apple blossom,
         up on the bank: the primroses!

D: Yes!

R: We picked a bunch
         on Mothering Sunday.

D: And then came the apple blossom.
         The boughs seemed laden down with it.

R: The fruit:
         Cox's Orange Pippins.

D: Are you sure?
         There were cooking apples as well.

R: And chickens pecking about
         under the trees.

D: You set fire to the chicken house.

R: Not deliberately.

D: Dad came and put the fire out

with a bucket of water.

R: It wasn't a big deal.

The Red Telephone Box

I'm in a telephone box.
I haven't got long,
The pips will start soon.

Why did you ring?

I rang to say I'm sorry.
I doubt I'll see you again.
I'm sorry
for the hurt I caused you.

pip, pip, pip.

Damn the pips,
this is my last shilling.

I can't hear you.
Did you say hurt?
What hurt?

I should have stood by you.
I just walked away.

pip, pip, pip.
peep

Oh
Damn the pips!

Sailing to the Isles of Scilly

"There are bad times just around the corner."
I'll take Noël Coward's advice and sail away
on the wings of the morning
with my own true love.

I'll heave on the twin halyards;
the great tan sail on its varnished spars
will rise above the white coach roof
to be silhouetted against a deep blue sky.

"Made!"
I'll call to the person on the helm.
We'll turn down wind.

The old boat gathers speed,
The noise of water against the hull quickens,
chuckling sounds become sloshing and slapping
as we greet the open sea,
leaving the smell of mud and seaweed behind.
Now there's a salty tang in the air,
spray stings my face.
"Westward Ho!"

The cold East Wind
will carry us down channel to the Isles of Scilly.
We'll stop each night in ancient ports.
There is no hurry:
lovers have all the time in the world.

In Weymouth,
we'll eat fish and chips in the cockpit.
At dawn we'll weigh anchor,
"Sunrise sparkles in your eyes, Lucy."

In Dartmouth,
we'll forge upriver to the Ferry Boat Inn.
We'll eat venison pie
with latter-day poachers and smugglers.

In Falmouth,
we'll join sailors singing sea chanties.

At last:
the Isles of Scilly,
we'll anchor off Hangman's Island.

The sun sets in crimson glory
behind a bank of clouds.
Beyond the clouds:
New York, New York!

Street Musician

(For Rémy)

He's playing a piece by Dire Straits,
strong beat, bouncy tune.
Amazing,
says my three year old grandson,
(it's his new word).
He starts to dance in jiggly steps,
perfectly in time with thump of the beat.
I'm carried away, not enough to dance
but I do reach deep into my pocket for a coin.

Then stand back and tap my foot.
The musician is all smiles and starts to dance too.
It's like they're riffing.
There's chemistry here,
some sort of primal response to the music
that transcends age, language and race.
It seems they are not going to stop.
Others join in.
Now there is a circle of people,
children and elders,
mothers and fathers,
all dancing in a ring.
In a moment the whole multitude is whirling around,
faster and faster,
so fast that their feet will leave the ground and
they will float over the roof of the cathedral,
and disappear behind the spire.

Tori
Learning to Ride

Toes up, hands down.
Kick on!
Choleric Colonel
slaps boot with whip,
and bellows commands.
Small agitated girl
flaps legs
in an effort
to make pony move.
Tweety Pie
remains
unimpressed
and
unmoving
until Laura (stable girl)
rattles
a bucket of horse nuts
from a corner of the field.
Sudden,
surprising
turn of speed,
deposits rider on the grass.
Here ends the lesson.

Tori
Hunter Trials

Laura (stable girl) helps me saddle up.
Dad ties number 23 onto my back.
He gives me a leg up.
Micky (Mercury VI to you)
does a quick pirouette,
I have to hold him in as
he sidles up to the start.
There's the gun!
We're away across the meadow.
The first few fences are straight forward.
Now it's the wood,
the stream
and a jump out
over post and rails.
This is where
Imogen and Prince
came unstuck.

Micky clears the fence,
we're back out in open fields.
Time counts so I reach forwards
over his neck.
"Go on Micky, go on!"
The last hedge flies past.
We're home.
Dad catches the bridle.
I dismount,
lead Micky back to the stables.
I pat him and rub him down.
Later,
still spattered with mud,
I collect a small silver cup
and a red rosette.
"Well done," says Dad.
Mum arrives,
she missed it all.
"I'm sorry I didn't watch you, darling."
I know they're proud of me,
they just don't like to show it.

Tori
The Hunt Ball

I felt unsure about dressing up.
I normally wear t-shirts and jeans
and when summer turns to autumn,
a thick woolly jumper.
Mum bought me a green satin dress.
It was tight,
cut square across the bust
and almost floor length.
"It matches your eyes," said Dad.
I was surprised.
He never normally notices things like that.

-§-

The Colonel and his wife were in the hall
welcoming guests.
He is now MFH.
(Master of Fox Hounds, just so you know.)
The Manor House is vast and cold.
But I had goose bumps already.
I stuck close to Mum,
She looked like my older sister
in a shimmering blue silk dress.

-§-

Then I saw Sally;
she was wearing lipstick!
"Oh Mum, please, please can I borrow yours?"

"NO."

"Dad, can you get the lip balm out of the car."
(Dad always does as I ask),
it is a bit shiny,
I'll bite my lips.
Then I hear Mum whisper to Dad:
"Sally's dressed up like a tart."
So Dad has to go over to her
and start talking about film stars
and a career on the stage.

-§-

Parents!
I need to break away
but I can't see how.
There are more families
arriving all the time.
We are being directed
through the drawing room
and out of the French Windows
into a huge marquee.
I've no choice
but to sit with my parents
feeling more and more like a gooseberry
in my green dress.

-§-

Then the dancing starts.
Sally and her friends

are doing what I imagine
is the Charleston,
but I can hardly move in this outfit,
in fact I have to waddle like a penguin.
I escape back into the drawing room,
hide behind a fire screen
and pretend to read Horse and Hound.
There Paul finds me
and lures me onto the dance floor
for a slow shuffle.
Then down the garden path
to the rose covered gazebo.

-§-

We're kissing
and I'm wondering
if I'm doing it right.
Paul is trying to undo
the hooks and eyes
on the back of my dress
but they are a like a dense hedge of thorns;
he has no chance of finding a way through.
Then he tries to put a hand up my skirt,
but it's so tight I couldn't get my knees apart
even if I wanted to.
All the time I'm keeping my eyes shut
and concentrating on kissing him.
"Let's go back to the dance," he says.
We return to the tent for another shuffle.

-§-

"It's time to go," says Dad.
Mum looks cross.
When I ask why,
Dad whispers that MFH
tried to pinch her bottom.
Why? I wonder,
but think it better not to ask.
I already know MFH has a thing going
with Laura (the stable girl).

-§-

Paul has disappeared.
I want to say goodbye.
We crunch across the gravel to the car.
Paul runs up behind us.
"I'm glad you came," he says.
"I so enjoyed our dance."
"Thank you for asking me," I reply.

-§-

So that was it my first ball.

MARIA
(notes for a novel)

Chapter One
From the very beginning.

I am good at history,
I was there,
from the very beginning.
I remember it all:
the ships on fire at Trafalgar,
Jeannette climbing from the stern window

of the burning Achilles.
The Scots Greys at Waterloo,
Lord Uxbridge losing his leg.
"My dancing days are over!"

My birth:
my mother's distress,
the Caesarean section.
Twins!
My brother and I,
have never been separated.
There was an operation,
but that was on my heart.
I was a blue baby.
I have had to struggle to keep up.

He's the athlete, tall and straight.
I'm not a cripple,
I've got two legs,
one shorter than the other,
that's all.

I like to scoot along.
On a scooter,
I look good.
On a horse,
I look wonderful.
I love my horse.

But I forgot to say:
I'm a girl, the second sex.
When I had a cardiac arrest,

after my first op,
I heard one doctors say.
"Never mind, the boy's alright."
The other doctor was leaning over me;
he had long greasy hair
tied back with a bow,
his lovely blue eyes,
crinkled up at the corners,
he said.
"She's alright,
just testing us out;
look, she's laughing."
I blew bubbles for him.
I love that man.
I love my brother.
I have long greasy hair now,
I tie it back with a bow.
I have lovely blue eyes.

Sometimes,
I am my brother.
It is something more than just pretending.
We are lookalikes,
Mother dressed us like identical twins.
"You are equals,
I love you both the same!"
When we started school,
our teacher could not tell us apart.
"Stop scooting!"
she would yell.

Chapter Two

Primary School

I told teacher:
"I can read. I don't need your help."
I turned the pages and chatted away.
It was a lovely story.

"Your daughter is so clever,
she can read already."
said the teacher.

"No she can't,"
said Mum.
"She just thinks she can.
You will have to teach her!"

But I was clever,
I am clever.
I learned all my lessons.
After a week,
I told Mum:
"I don't need to go to school anymore,
There is nothing more they can teach me."

Mum was not amused,
"You will go to school.
It's the law of the land."

Chapter Three

In the Playground

"Why do you walk like that?" Craig asked.
His friends giggled.
"I've got a stone in my shoe," I lied.
But they didn't go away,
they kept on about my limp.
I slapped the big bully.
He hit me back.
Rick jumped on him.
They rolled in the dirt.
Alec went to help Craig but
I kicked him on the shin and he fell over.

Teacher was cross.
"I had to kick him,
because he was going to hurt Rick," I explained.
She didn't seem to understand.

Chapter Four

Games.

I don't do games.
I am athletic,
but I don't play hockey or lacrosse.
And I don't do gym.
Mum arranged for me to have piano lessons
when the others had gym.
On Wednesday afternoons,
when others played games,
I went riding.

The teasing didn't stop,
being special probably made it worse,
but I liked my music and riding lessons.
I liked to show off.
School concerts were great.
Gymkhanas were even better.

Chapter Five

Horses

Rick loves horses too;
at first we had to share.
Mum soon realised her mistake;
she sold all her jewels to buy us one each.

Mine was a strawberry roan called
Bonnie Prince Charlie or Bonnie for short.
His was a grey welsh mountain called
Misty Morning or Misty for short.
We spent hours in the stables mucking out.
Together,
we would gallop across the Downs.

Chapter Six

Senior School

Rick went away to boarding school.
Misty was sold.
I went to a school run by Nuns.
It wasn't a convent,
I was allowed to take Bonnie with me.
I was sad.
I didn't like being a girl.
Boobs, periods were not for me.
Make up made no sense.
I wanted to be just like Rick.
Just like when we went to our first school.
I stopped eating.
Then the nuns told me about the Virgin Mary.
Maria.
We have the same name.
We have the same blue eyes.
When I told Rick he said:
"No: her eyes were brown or maybe green when she
was angry"
"But Sister Jane has seen Her in a vision and She had
the most wonderful blue eyes."
I stopped telling Rick about Maria.
I became saintly.
I fasted and wore only a simple shirt,
whatever the weather.

Chapter Seven

School Holidays

Dad was shocked.
Mum was furious.
Rick burst into tears.
"What has happened to you?" he asked.
Dad said nothing.
Mum knew exactly what the problem was:
"It's those Nuns."
Rick borrowed Emma's horse.
We went riding up on the Downs.
We sang, we laughed.
I started eating.
Rick laughed and kissed me.
"You're eating like a horse," said Dad.
"You're not going back to that school," said Mum.
"I love you Santa Maria," said Rick,
"Don't blaspheme. I still love the Virgin Mary."
"So do I," said Rick.

Chapter Eight

The Virgin Mary

Rick started collecting pictures of the Virgin Mary.
Pictures by Renaissance artists.
Pictures of the models that those artists used.
Some with clothes,
some without.
He called them all Maria.
The ones clothed were plastered
over his bedroom walls at home,
and his study at school.
The naked ones were kept in a secret folder.
He and I used to look at the images.
"Isn't she beautiful?" he asked.
He was looking at a painting
by Lucas Cranach the Elder.
"Such small boobs!" I said.
"Like yours, Maria, but yours are more beautiful."
Alone in my room
I looked at myself in the full length mirror.
I was standing naked in front of the glass.
"I am beautiful," I said to myself.
In walked Rick.
He fell to his knees.
"Maria,
you've become a goddess."

Chapter Nine

Maria Gets Sick

I was always a sickly child.
I was born with a heart that was not formed properly.
I had operations.
The surgeon was pleased.
I played with the others in the playground.
I rode my pony at Gymkhanas,
but I was prone to blue spells.
My heart might suddenly beat very fast.
I might faint.
I grew up into a tall, thin, beautiful teenager.

Rick adored me,
even worshipped me.

Then he started at Medical School.

That was when I became breathless.
The surgeon was anxious:
"We must operate."
He always used the Royal We.
"First we must do the tests,
and scan your heart,"
said the doctor with the long greasy hair.

Chapter Ten

On the Waiting List

Rick takes up the story.

Maria was in hospital.
Her heart was slowly failing.
No operation would help.
The last chance was a heart transplant.
We would have to wait.
I spent hours by her bedside holding her hand,
reading to her.
Mum and Dad came and went.
Days and weeks came and went.
Maria became weaker and more breathless.
She collapsed forwards over her table,
or leant back, propped up on pillows,
never comfortable,
never able to breath easily.
"Let me take her home," I begged the doctors.
Maria wanted to go home.
Mum and Dad agreed.

Chapter Eleven

At Home

The end had come.
We gathered round her bed.
We never left her.
Days passed.
Nights passed.

Then one evening as it grew dusk,
when we were alone,
she whispered.
"I am going now.
You will spend the rest of your life looking for me.
I am the one true love you can never have.
I am Maria."

Maria smiled.
She stopped breathing.

Rick

I had to forget Maria
and concentrate on my studies,
but it was impossible.
I found myself talking to her all the time.
I explained things to her
and revised things with her.
She always seemed to understand
what I was saying.
That didn't surprise me.
She was clever.
I came to accept
she was always going to be with me.
In that sense she never died.

THE END

Postscript.

Many of these poems were first read out loud at the Wagtail Coffee House, in Chichester, at open-mic meetings arranged by Words Out Loud and led by Ken Jones and team. I am grateful for all their kind help and encouragement.

wordsoutloud.org.uk

Printed in Great Britain
by Amazon

18924939R00031